CW00516410

James Rae

38 More Modern Studies for Solo Clarinet

James Rae, 38 More Modern Studies for Solo Clarinet

Cover Design: Lynette Williamson

UE 21554
ISMN 979-0-008-08345-7
UPC 8-03452-06723-8
ISBN 978-3-7024-7014-2

Inhalt / Contents / Table des matières

1. Horizon 2
2. Windsor March 2
3. Waves 2
4. Hungarian Lament 3
5. Intermezzo 3
6. Entomology 4
7. The Organ Grinder's Apprentice 4
8. The Middle Man 5
9. The Sheriff 5
10. Diversion 6
11. Ups and Downs 6
12. Blue Waltz 7
13. Destiny 7
14. The Swinger 8
15. Staccato Dance 8
16. Pieces of Eight 8
17. Lucky Number 9
18. Olympic Flame 10
19. Rock Summit 10
20. Straight Five 11
21. Swing Five 12
22. Odd Waltz 12
23. Exhibit A 13
24. Late Train Blues 14
25. 5th Avenue 15
26. Black Puddin' Jig 16
27. Hot Noodles 17
28. Journeys 18
29. Talkin' the Talk 19
30. The Funkmeister 20
31. Breakaway 21
32. And Your Time Starts Now! 22
33. Loops 23
34. Coastal Reflections 24
35. Fairground Waltz 25
36. Tongue Twister 26
37. New Work 29
38. Hocus Pocus 30

Preface

This book was written in the same format as *40 Modern Studies for Clarinet*. Again, the pieces are of moderate length and cover a wide variety of styles. As the studies are technically demanding, they are all written in comfortable clarinet-orientated keys to allow the student to focus on interpretation. Each study is designed to improve the student's musical as well as technical abilities.

James Rae, November 2010

Vorwort

Dieses Buch wurde im gleichen Stil wie *40 Modern Studies for Clarinet* geschrieben. Die Etüden sind relativ kurz und umfassen eine bunte Auswahl verschiedenster Stilrichtungen. Da die Studien technisch anspruchsvoll sind, stehen sie alle in für die Klarinette geeigneten Tonlagen und erlauben den SpielerInnen damit, sich auf die Interpretation zu konzentrieren. So bietet jede Etüde die Möglichkeit, die musikalischen und technischen Fähigkeiten zu verbessern.

James Rae, November 2010

Préface

Ce recueil s'inscrit dans la lignée des *40 Modern Studies for Clarinet*, avec là encore des pièces d'une durée modérée et d'une grande diversité de styles. Compte tenu de leur difficulté technique, les pièces sont toutes écrites dans des tonalités confortables pour la clarinette, afin d'encourager l'élève à se concentrer sur l'interprétation. Chaque étude est conçue pour permettre à l'élève d'améliorer ses compétences techniques et musicales.

James Rae, novembre 2010

1. Horizon

James Rae
(*1957)

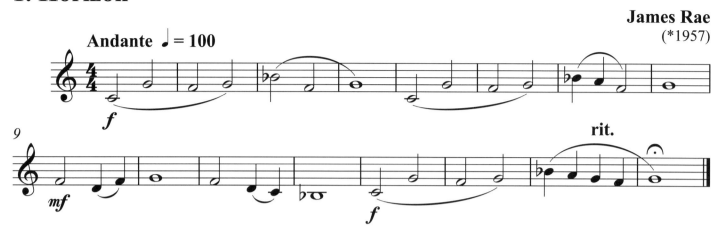

2. Windsor March

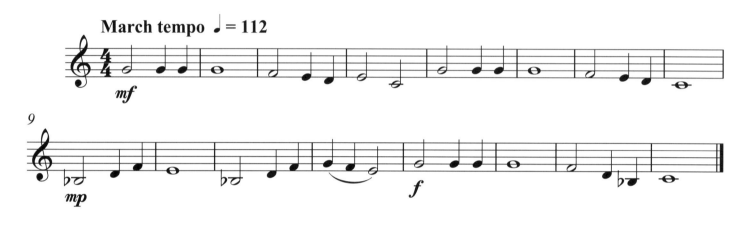

3. Waves

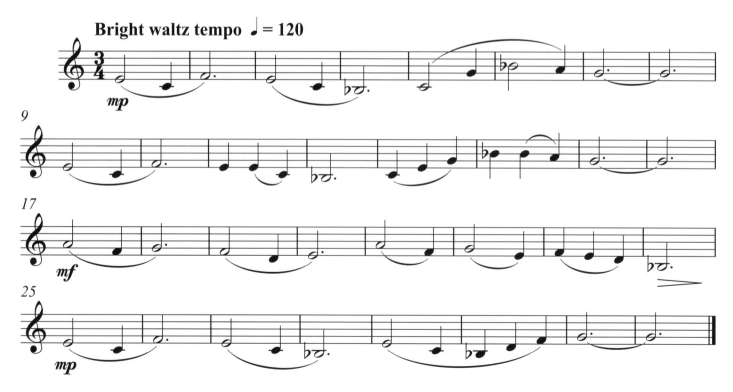

Universal Edition UE 21 554

4. Hungarian Lament

5. Intermezzo

UE 21 554

4

6. Entomology

7. The Organ Grinder's Apprentice

UE 21 554

8. The Middle Man

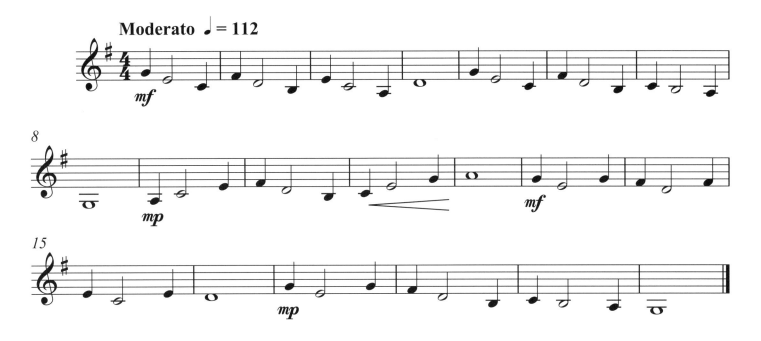

9. The Sheriff

UE 21554

10. Diversion

11. Ups and Downs

UE 21 554

12. Blue Waltz

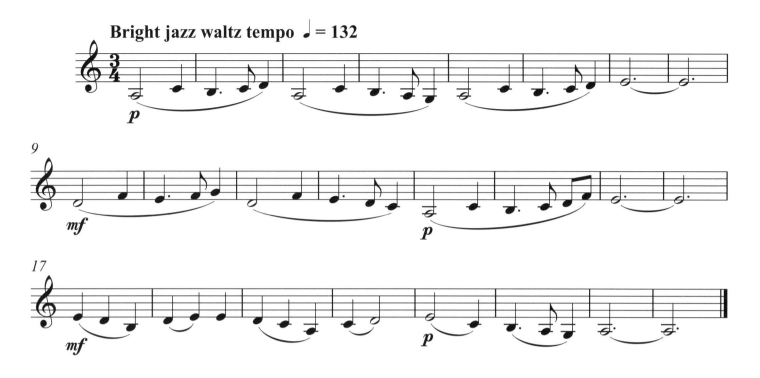

13. Destiny

UE 21 554

14. The Swinger

15. Staccato Dance

16. Pieces of Eight

UE 21 554

17. Lucky Number

UE 21 554

18. Olympic Flame

19. Rock Summit

UE 21 554

20. Straight Five

UE 21 554

21. Swing Five

22. Odd Waltz

UE 21 554

23. Exhibit A

UE 21 554

24. Late Train Blues

UE 21 554

25. 5th Avenue

UE 21 554

26. Black Puddin' Jig

UE 21554

27. Hot Noodles

Bright bebop tempo ♩ = 200+ (swing quavers)

UE 21 554

28. Journeys

Lento espressivo ♩ = 60

UE 21 554

29. Talkin' the Talk

UE 21 554

20

30. The Funkmeister

Solid funk tempo ♩ = 108

UE 21 554

31. Breakaway

Cool bossa nova feel ♩ = 120

UE 21 554

32. And Your Time Starts Now!

Strict and mechanical ♩ = 120

UE 21 554

33. Loops

* Play each repeat at least four times. / *Jede Wiederholung ist mindestens vier Mal zu spielen.* /
  Jouer les passages avec barre de reprise au moins quatre fois.

UE 21 554

34. Coastal Reflections

UE 21 554

35. Fairground Waltz

Bright waltz tempo ♩ = 148+

UE 21 554

36. Tongue Twister

Vivo ♩ = 120

mf leggiero

pp

mp

mf

pp

UE 21 554

37. New Work

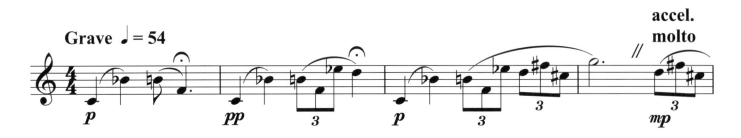

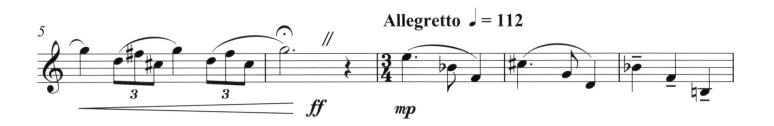

UE 21 554

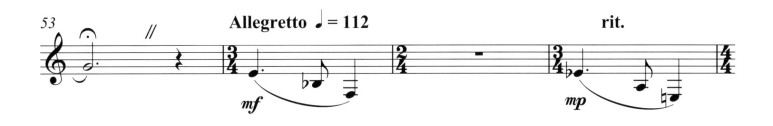

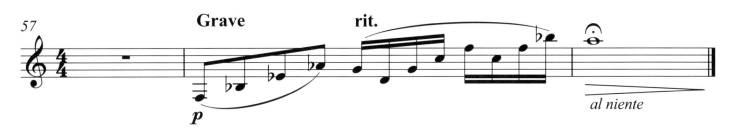

UE 21 554

38. Hocus Pocus

UE 21 554

UE 21 554

Clarinet Albums and Tutors
in Lighter Styles

■ EASY

James Rae • Introducing the Clarinet Plus Book 1 (clar. & pno) * • UE 30 422

■ EASY TO INTERMEDIATE

James Rae • Introducing the Clarinet (Engl.) (clar. & CD) • UE18 780

James Rae • James Rae's Methode für Klarinette (Dt.) (Klar. & CD) • UE 31 286

James Rae • Introducing the Clarinet Plus Book 2 (clar. & pno) • UE 30 423

James Rae • Introducing Clarinet – Duets (2 clar.) • UE 21 310

James Rae • Introducing Clarinet – Trios (3 clar.) • UE 21 311

James Rae • Introducing Clarinet – Quartets (4 clar.) • UE 21 312

James Rae • Style Workout – Clarinet (clar.) • UE 21 301

■ INTERMEDIATE

Take Ten (clar. & pno) *arr. James Rae* • UE 19 736

Take Another Ten (clar. & pno) *arr. James Rae* • UE 21 169

Scott Joplin • 5 Rags (clar. & pno) *arr. James Rae* • UE 19 661

James Rae • Jazz Zone – Clarinet (clar. & CD) • UE 21 031

Kurt Weill • 6 Pieces From The Threepenny Opera (2 clar. & pno)

arr. James Rae • UE 31 181

Kurt Weill • Music From The Threepenny Opera (4 clar. or 3 clar. & bass clar.)

arr. James Rae • UE 30 117

■ WORLD MUSIC PLAY-ALONG (clar. & CD, pno. ad lib.)

Yale Strom • Klezmer • UE 31 569

Israel *arr. Timna Brauer & Elias Meiri* • UE 31 555

Diego Collatti • Argentina • UE 31 566

Russia *arr. Ivan Malachovsky* • UE 31 557

Jovino Santos Neto • Brazil • UE 31 562

Ireland *arr. Richard Graf* • UE 31 575